CRACKED

A Snack-Sized Mystery

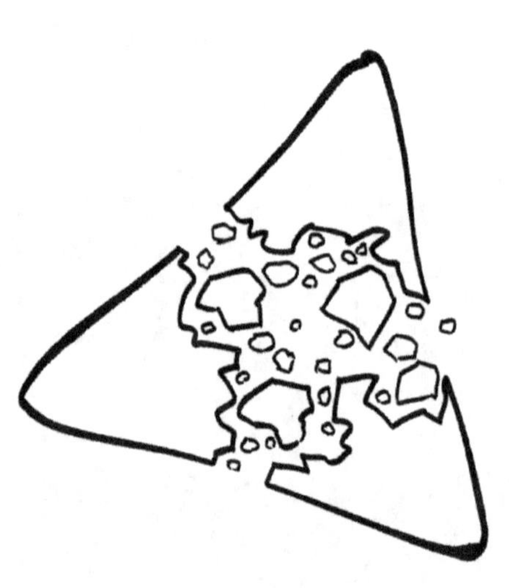

CRACKED

A Snack-Sized Mystery

Jeff Schmoyer

Jmars Ink

Art by Ani Sledgianowski

Published by Jmars Ink
Visit JmarsInk.com

ISBN 979-8-9881866-1-8

Acknowledgments

A feast of thanks to my fabulous beta readers
Deborah L Brewer and Robert Spiller.

Chapter One

I schlepped to my regular Sunday brunch place, Fash Food, and was greeted by Rudy at the host stand out front, by the sidewalk.

"Good morning, sir!" he said. "We have your favorite table available if you would like to sit on the patio on this fine day."

"Perfect, but please, call me Murph—the king has not anointed me, yet."

I followed him inside the iron fence to the flagstone-paved patio. My usual table was off to one side, away from the door, amid flowering hedges. This day, it was the only table still in the glaring sun.

"Rudy, would you mind if I opened the umbrella over the table?"

"Let me get it. I can't imagine why it's the only one that's still closed." Rudy struggled with the crank on the oversized umbrella. "It seems to be stuck."

"That's okay," I said. "I can sit at another table today."

"No, I'll get it."

With a final shove of the crank handle, the umbrella popped fully open, dropping a dead body onto my table.

Chapter Two

My friend, Dave, put his gloved fingers on the neck of the body that lay on the table where I had been hoping to have my breakfast served.

"As expected, he's deceased," Dave said. "How many does this make, Murph?"

"That's not nice, Dave."

"Well, it's got to be double digits by now." Dave reached into the dead man's pants pockets and set the contents on the table.

"I can't help it if people keep turning up dead around me. You're keeping count?"

"As my job is medical examiner, yes, I keep count." He opened the man's wallet. Inside was a little cash and a bus pass, but no ID.

"Well, as a humble food blogger, I don't." *At least not off the top of my head.* I could go back and count them in my blog posts.

"And yet, here we are again. Do you know this guy?"

This guy, as Dave called him, was dressed in well-worn jeans and a work shirt. His face was blistered and swollen. He could have been Dave, and I wouldn't have been able to tell. I shook my head.

Rudy, Fash Food's host, stepped from the crowd gathered outside the iron fence to address Dave. "How much longer should I tell people we'll be closed?"

"At least the rest of the day. Don't let anybody leave, though. When the police arrive, they'll want to talk to each of them."

"Rudy, would you please get me a pastry?" I hadn't had so much as a cup of coffee yet.

"Of course, sir."

"How can you eat with a dead body lying here?" Dave mocked.

"I'll eat it over there." I motioned past the fence. "I thought you were still on vacation, or I would have invited you to join me this morning."

"I got back last night, good thing. I heard the call on the radio and came over to see if you were here. You know, this is your usual table."

"Yeah?"

"Somebody leaves you a corpse and you don't think it's strange?"

"I don't think everything is about me."

Rudy came up and handed me a banana. *Had he been talking to my doctor?* I ate it while I waited for the police to arrive and take my statement.

Chapter Three

Since brunch had been a bust and it was almost lunchtime, I walked a couple of blocks east to a lesser choice in Sunday dining, Penumbra. The repurposed old house smelled of burnt toast and bacon and was packed, with still more people waiting out front to get in. My Pavlovian response to the aroma of bacon kept me from walking on.

Someone was frantically waving to me from his table inside. Unfortunately for me, Gary saw that he had caught my eye. I cut through the crowd at the door.

"Murphy," he said. "Come, sit. How long has it been?"

Not nearly long enough. But I knew I was playing with fire coming to this place. I was in desperate need of coffee by then, and maybe that had kept me from thinking straight. I sat down across from him.

"Thanks, Gary," I said. "This place sure is busy today."

"More so than even the usual weekend crowds. They're down a cook, plus I heard that Fash Food is closed today."

Great—the service would be even slower than usual. It might be a good day to start my diet. Before I could get up, the smiling chef/owner of the place was tableside.

"Mr. Murphy! I'm so glad you've decided to join us. My two favorite local restaurant critics on my busiest day—how lucky can I get? My previous offer stands—anything you want on the house."

"I appreciate the offer, Burke," I said, "but I like to pay my own way. Besides, I'm not here to do a review."

His smile disappeared. "Oh."

Gary jumped in, "I'll do a review! Put Murphy's breakfast on my tab."

Yes, Gary was my competition, so to speak. Though this town was plenty big enough for more than one food critic, I didn't like his style, nor was it evident that he had ever paid for a meal in his life. I was pretty sure he wouldn't be paying for my meal, either.

"You know, I'm not feeling all that well. I should go home." It wasn't a lie. I had the start of a headache—all I had consumed all day was a banana, and no coffee.

Chef Burke said, "Please stay, Mr. Murphy. Today's special will make you feel so much better you won't be able to resist giving it a rave review."

The thought of spending more time with Gary made me even more ill, but I gave in. "Fine. I'll have the special. And coffee."

"I'll have the special, too," Gary said. "And a side of bacon, and a couple of those cinnamon rolls you know I like."

Two cinnamon rolls? If memory served, those things were huge.

Burke nodded and walked away, scribbling on his pad. Now it was just me and Gary and my flip-flopping belly. Fortunately, the coffee and pastries showed up right away—Gary even offered me one of the cinnamon rolls. Sugar, butter, cinnamon, warm—I could see why he would order two.

Chapter Four

The next morning, my ringing phone caught me staring at an empty blog page. The special at Penumbra had been nothing to write home, or a blog post, about—Gary probably had it covered anyway.

"Hi, Dave," I said to my savior on the other end of the call.

"Hi, Murph. How are you holding up?"

"Sadly, it's not my first dead body. Anything you can tell me about him?"

"The cause of death was a blow to the back of the head with a flat object, something like a coal shovel."

"What was up with his face?" I grimaced, having that image once again come into focus.

"Severe burns—possibly to keep him from being identified. His fingerprints aren't in the system."

"So, no way to ID him?"

"I didn't say that. We have a name, which, before you ask, I can't tell you until we find his family and notify them."

I had an idea how they had found his name. "It was the bus pass, wasn't it?"

"Yes, you're an excellent detective, for a food blogger. I'll let you know more when I can. In the meantime, try to stay out of trouble."

"Tell trouble to stop looking for me. Thanks for calling, Dave."

I set to work on a blog post about the previous morning's non-breakfast.

Chapter Five

I was a few minutes early for my regular massage appointment. The door to the private room was closed so I waited my turn in the small lobby and debated whether I needed a cup of complimentary coffee from the single-serve machine. Before I could finish weighing the pros and cons of yet another cup of joe that day, I heard Steph go into the massage room.

Even though she had closed the door behind her, I could still hear her voice. "Your time is up, Mr. McCloud. I have another client so you can't nap any longer today. Mr. McCloud."

Usually, I couldn't hear what was going on in the room where it happened. After a third, even louder "Mr. McCloud," I knocked on the door.

"Steph, is everything okay?"

"Murph? I'm sorry for the delay. I can't seem to wake my last client."

I opened the door and barged in. A heavyset, mostly bald man, covered to his shoulders by a sheet, lay face down on the massage table. I placed my hand on his neck and looked back to a concerned massage therapist.

"I'm afraid Mr. McCloud won't be getting up from his nap today, Steph."

"No. That can't be. Mr. McCloud?" she cried once more.

"Help me flip him over and I'll start chest compressions. Then you need to call 911."

I threw off the sheet and was relieved the man was wearing shorts. We flipped him over, then Steph left the room to make the call.

Happy not to have to give mouth-to-mouth to the bearded man, I performed cardiac presses until the paramedics got there and took over. They slid the man onto a stretcher and took him away.

"Do you think he'll be alright?" Steph asked.

I didn't want to tell her the truth—Mr. McCloud would never need another massage.

"I'm sure they'll do everything they can for him," I offered.

"Give me a minute to change the sheets, and we can get you onto the table."

"Steph, I think we should reschedule. How about you sit down with me and tell me what happened."

"What happened? With Mr. McCloud? It was a regular massage like you get."

I sat down in the empty lobby and she reluctantly joined me.

"Did he seem okay when he came in today?" I asked.

"He said he wasn't feeling well, but that he would be fine if he could lie down, so I just went with it."

"Did he often take a nap afterward?" If this was a thing, I needed to know about it.

"Sometimes, when I didn't have another client right away." She stood up. "I understand if you don't want a massage today, we can reschedule. Let me go clean up the room so it will be ready for tomorrow."

"I don't think you should touch anything in there."

"Is there something you're trying to tell me, Murph?"

"You should close and go home for the day. Finding Mr. McCloud like that can be traumatic."

She didn't seem to get it, and I wasn't sure I did either. This was the second body that I had crossed paths with in as many days. The first death certainly wasn't by natural causes, and I feared this one wasn't either.

Chapter Six

It wasn't long before my phone alerted me that my presence was required at the local police station. I wasn't sure which fatality they wanted to talk to me about. The answer, of course, was both.

When I arrived, the detective got right to it. "Mr. Murphy, you had an appointment after a Conor McCloud at All Hands on Back, correct?"

"Yes, detective. I was there earlier today."

"Please talk me through it."

I told him exactly what had happened and where I was before and after, to be thorough.

When my story was done and notes were taken, he asked, "Did you know Mr. McCloud?"

"I did not. Have you talked to Steph yet?"

"The massage therapist? I'll be meeting with her shortly."

"Mind if I join you?"

"Yes, I do mind."

Well, it didn't hurt to ask. So I continued asking. "What happened to Mr. McCloud?"

"Mr. McCloud is dead."

"What did he die from? It looks like you're investigating a homicide. I told you what I knew—tell me what's going on."

"Mr. Murphy, you know it doesn't work that way."

"And you know I'll find out what's up pretty quick, so let's skip to the chase."

He gave up. "We are treating this as a suspicious death. We're waiting on the autopsy results to determine the cause."

Interesting. "Is that all you need from me?"

"I also want to ask you about the victim you found at Fash Food yesterday."

"The man in the umbrella?"

"Yes, the man in the umbrella. Did you know him?"

"No, I didn't know him, either, though the damage to his face makes it a little hard to tell if I'd seen him around somewhere." I had already answered these questions at the scene, but I knew how this worked from past experience. "Dave said you were able to ID him."

"Dave said that, did he?"

Uh, oh. I hoped I hadn't gotten Dave in trouble, or worse. "He didn't tell me who he was or anything."

The detective disregarded my imprudence. "Tell me about yesterday morning."

He scribbled on his pad while I revisited the events aloud.

Then I took another shot with my own questions. "Were you able to talk to his family? Did you find out anything about him or where he worked?"

The detective gave me a look that said he would like me to leave now. But I stayed.

He sighed. "We did speak to someone, but it was a dead end."

That wasn't worth staying for. He stood, indicating once again that he was done with me. This time, I took him up on the offer to skedaddle.

Chapter Seven

There was a knock at my front door as I pulled the sheet pan from the oven. I set it onto the cooling rack and went to see who had a nose for fresh cookies.

I opened the front door a crack, and a small, furry critter squeezed in and ran past me.

Not another raccoon—when did they learn to knock?

The front door was pushed open further, and a larger creature in bright plumage rushed by.

"Murphy, come back here!" the larger beast shouted.

"Kimber?" I stammered.

She scooped up her wayward pup. "Hi, Murph. How have you been?"

"I've been fine. What are you doing here?"

"I flew in to help."

"Help with what?"

"The murders," she announced, setting her large purse on my sofa.

"How do you know about the murders?"

"Your blog, of course—you write about everything."

I had mentioned them in my blog. Not too many details—I didn't want to interfere with the police investigations.

"Don't forget, I helped you with that other case," she continued.

"Helped me? You were more suspect than assistant."

"Come on. You didn't really believe I was the killer, did you?" She batted her long eyelashes at me.

And, yeah, I did really believe she could have done it. But she hadn't. We parted ways after and I hadn't even thought about her since.

I asked, "How did you find me? I certainly don't post where I live on my blog."

"It's easy to tell you're from Colorado from all the local restaurant reviews. The Secretary of State's website has your business address, which I assumed was also your home address—and it was."

Indeed, it was. She showed some detective skills. But I still didn't want her assistance.

"I don't need any help, Kimber. I'm not investigating the murders. Besides, the second man's death might not even be a murder. The police have it well in hand."

"Do they have any suspects?"

"I don't think so, but it's early days. You should go back to wherever it is you came from."

"Two dead bodies placed right where *you* would find them, and you're not looking into them? That doesn't sound like the food-blogging detective I know."

"I don't think you know me all that well." But she made a good point. Both bodies were put along my path. *This wasn't about me, as Dave had suggested, was it?* It was a lousy frame job if that was the intent.

"Are those fresh-baked cookies I smell?" She started towards my kitchen.

I hung my head—she wasn't going away. "Care for some tea?"

I put down a bowl of water for her pooch, then we sat at the counter and ate warm cookies from the cooling rack—the very best way to do it—while we sipped our hot tea.

"These are extremely chocolatey and cinnamon-y," Kimber said. "And something else…"

"Ginger. I wanted a bit of heat but was out of cayenne pepper."

"Nice. I'll have to steal the recipe."

"I'll post it to my blog."

She had mentioned during our previous encounter, more than once, that she had received an enormous sum in her divorce, giving her the freedom to do things like show up on my front porch, unannounced. As the food-blogging detective, I was a little nosy. "Do you mind if I ask what your ex-husband did for a living?"

"He was in the furniture business. But his claim to fame and fortune came from inventing the Quing bed."

"The what?"

She took a sip of tea and leaned back on her stool. "You know how sometimes a queen-size bed feels too small when you have a partner, but when you're in a king-size bed you might never be able to find them? That's the problem the Quing bed solved. It was genius. My ex called it the king of queen beds."

"For real?" I reached for another cookie.

"Oh, yeah. He sold the patent to one of the big mattress companies. Since I had helped him test them for years, I got half in the divorce."

"That is…unexpected."

"Let me know if you want one—I can get you a discount."

"I think I'm good right now." My queen bed served me just fine, seeing as I was partnerless.

"Did you know umbrella guy?" Kimber asked.

"Is that what we're calling him?"

"If we don't know his name, we need to call him something."

I didn't like to be disrespectful of the dead, especially those dead at the hands of someone else, but referring to him as John Doe wasn't any better. "I didn't know umbrella guy, as far as I could tell—he was a little hard to identify. And before you ask, I didn't know massage guy."

"You don't know his name, either?" she asked.

"Oh, I do—it's Conor McCloud. We should call him that." I slurped up the rest of my tea. "So, as you can see, there is nothing for you, or me, to do here. Thanks for the visit. Stay safe on your trip back home."

"This town looks like a delightful place to spend a few days. I'll be at the B&B on 26th if you need me."

"I won't need you."

After she left, I surveyed what remained of the cookies, then pulled the flour back out of the pantry.

Pro tip: Trap the tag on a tea bag under the bottom edge of the cup so that it doesn't jump in when you pour the hot water from the kettle. Bonus tip: Always bake extra cookies.

Chapter Eight

The following morning, I went out back to the garage to get Irma, my classic car, to take me to lunch downtown. After a quick look into the void, I remembered I had left her by the curb out front as I'd had an issue with the garage door the night before. My neighborhood was safe-ish, as long as you didn't leave anything in the car, which I usually didn't.

Arriving out front at Irma, I found there was something left behind—well, not something, but someone. I hoped it was a homeless person asleep in the passenger seat. I knocked gently on the window and looked closer. The pair of scissors sticking from her chest told me I would get no response.

An hour later, a tow truck carted Irma away as evidence. Kimber was right—the murders were definitely about me. I was unknowingly complicit in the deaths of three people I didn't recognize. This was a new low in my life.

After another hour of moping, I called my ME friend Dave to see what he could tell me about the latest victim. "Hi, Dave, it's Murph."

"Hi, Murph. I can't talk."

"I know you're busy. Sorry about that."

"No, Murph. I'm not allowed to talk to you anymore. That last murder was too close. I'm not saying you're a suspect, yet. I've got to go."

"I understand. Bye, Dave."

Now I felt even worse.

The victim in my car cinched it—someone was murdering people because of me. And I had no idea why. Or how to make it stop. The police didn't seem to have a clue either, at least not one they wanted to share with me. Regardless of what I had told Kimber, I would have to investigate.

Or run.

Maybe that was the best idea—leave town. Escape to somewhere no one could find me and leave me another corpse. Then there would be no point to continued killings and they would stop.

I got started packing but then remembered that Irma was AWOL. I couldn't go anywhere until the police released her, and that might be long after the killer was caught.

Maybe my blog was the problem. Perhaps someone didn't like what I had to say. I wrote more than restaurant reviews. How could I find out whom I had alienated?

I looked over the last couple of blog posts—there was a new comment on the one about my finding umbrella guy that I hadn't seen. All it said was:

DO YOUR JOB

All caps and shouty. A comment on the post about the second victim made the same point with extra emphasis:

DO. YOUR. JOB.

I wasn't sure what to make of them. Did they mean I needed to solve the murders faster? That wasn't really my job. Were they from the murderer? Did they want to be caught?

I needed to end this. My finger hovered over the mouse button, ready to click my blog into oblivion. It would be final. The screen said there would be no turning back.

Murphy Slaw had been my career—my life—for more years than I could calculate in my current state of mind. It was also my main source of revenue, the rest being newspaper and magazine review columns. Those would have to stop, too, if I were to erase my footprint on the chance the killings would stop.

No more income—I would have to get a real job. I had given up on those as quickly as I could make a living wage from eating and writing about it. But now I would need to find something low-profile, out of the limelight. Maybe I could sell Quing beds.

I glanced out my front window. There was a car parked at the curb—with another body in it.

Chapter Nine

I flew out the front door, pulling out my phone to call 911 as I ran. Before I could dial, I saw the body move—she was still alive. As I got to the side of the car, I could see, "Kimber? What in the world are you doing? You nearly scared me half to death!"

"Oh, sorry. I was giving Murphy a bite to eat before we came to see you."

I stood at the side of her car, bent over with my hands on my knees—I wasn't much of a runner.

"What's wrong, Murph?" she asked.

"There's been another murder," I panted.

"I didn't see it in your blog."

"I'm done with my blog." It made sense—I should stop writing, at least until the killer was caught.

"How can I help?" she asked.

My head was spinning. "I don't know. I only know I have to stop the killings somehow."

After I had mostly recovered from my short sprint, we went inside my house and I told her about the latest murder and showed her the comments on the recent blog posts.

"Did you tell the police about these?" she asked.

"No, not yet." It was a good thing I hadn't deleted my blog. I really hadn't been thinking clearly.

I sent Dave a message about the comments. Hopefully the police could figure out who posted them.

Kimber said, "How about if you take me through exactly what happened in each case and we'll try to come up with a plan."

Surprisingly, it made me feel better that she would be helping me.

She attached her furry companion's leash and we walked by the park on the way to the first crime scene. The park was home to several food trucks that day. While Murphy sniffed the greenery, Kimber and I played a little game to take my mind off my current plight, at least momentarily.

"That truck is called Guac in the Park," I said to her, pointing to a bright green mobile food dispensary. What do you think is their specialty?"

She answered promptly and correctly, "Avocado toast, if that's still a thing."

"It still tastes good, in any case. Next up—Sno Regrets." I pointed to a trailer with a winter mountain scene on the side.

"I would guess shave ice, but I don't get the regrets," she said.

"Hawaiian shave ice is correct. The owners tell me that Colorado is no substitute for Hawaii." *Hmm, Maui could be a nice place to run away to.*

I noticed Kimber squinting in the bright sunshine at another truck.

"Bacon Express," she read aloud. "It sounds right up your alley."

I took her arm and moved her so she could get a better view. "Read it again."

"Oh. Bacon Excess. That is totally you."

Scrawled on a piece of paper stuck in the food truck's window was, "Closed." *No bacon for us today.*

We continued strolling west till we got to Fash Food.

"I know this place from the description on your blog," Kimber said. "It's your favorite Sunday brunch stop."

"It was."

Fash Food had returned to service, sans my usual table and its umbrella, that area cordoned off with police tape. The crime scene delineation didn't stop a few customers from partaking in afternoon drinks on the patio. Rudy didn't seem to be around to fork over anything he might have learned in the interim.

I told Kimber about the missing table and large umbrella, and went into as much detail as I could remember about the sudden appearance of the first victim. It was getting to be kind of a blur as I was in three bodies deep. I needed to keep it all fresh to help solve the string of murders as quickly as possible.

"What did you do after?" she asked.

"I was still hungry and in desperate need of coffee so I walked down the street to Penumbra."

"Maybe you can take me there later?"

"Maybe. In the meantime, the next stop is All Hands on Back, the massage therapy place. That's where I found the second victim." We crossed at the corner and turned east.

Kimber prompted Murphy to move along from a lamp post. "How did the killer know you would show up there?"

"I'm not sure. I was a regular and had an appointment. They could have seen my name on the calendar?"

"Whose calendar, the shop's or yours?"

"Good question." *Had I been hacked?* I kept all my appointments on an online calendar. Things were just getting worse.

Chapter Ten

The door to the massage studio was unlocked, so we walked right in. Steph was nowhere in sight and the therapy room looked the same as when I last saw it, other than the sheets being gone.

Kimber set Murphy onto the massage table to keep him safely out of the way as we inspected the small room. While it was compact, there were lots of potions, tools of the trade, and small appliances lining the walls. There was a crock pot full of stones, clean towels, a basket for used towels, and a jacket on the coat rack. *Could the jacket belong to the ill-fated Mr. McCloud?* Before rifling through the pockets, I checked on my helpers.

Kimber was nosing around the room, and her scruffy companion was doing the same on the massage table. He worked his way up to the face cradle at the head end of the table. I snatched him up off the table right before his tongue removed some possible evidence.

"Kimber, I think your little gumshoe may have found a clue."

I handed her dog to her and bent down to examine the face cradle.

"What do you see, Murph?"

"It looks like there is a small smear of something brownish." I gave it a quick sniff.

Kimber pushed me aside and took her own whiff. "Peanut butter?"

"It could be," I speculated. "Could McCloud have had a nut allergy? Steph said he didn't feel well when he arrived."

"Might your friend, Dave, be able to tell you?"

"Maybe..." *If we were talking.* "In the meantime, I need to speak with Steph."

"Okay. I'll reward Murphy with a trip outdoors."

I found Steph in the back.

"Oh, hi, Murph. Did I forget about your appointment?" she asked.

"No, though I still need to make a new one. Can you tell me if Mr. McCloud had any allergies?"

"Not that I know of. Why?"

I was afraid I was reaching for any straw I could grasp, but if this was a crime scene, I had to get it sealed. "I need to call the police and tell them about something I found. Can we lock the massage room until they get here?"

"Murph, this is my livelihood. Mr. McCloud's unfortunate death has already cost me business. I've had several cancellations since the word got out. Please don't make this harder on me."

My life was crashing, and now I was taking Steph's down as well. I could turn and walk away from all of it—leave Steph alone. But that wasn't me.

"I'm sorry, Steph. But if there's a serial killer out there, the police will need all the evidence they can get to pursue them."

"A serial killer?" She looked terrified.

Somehow, I had made this even worse.

Chapter Eleven

I met Kimber out front and filled her in on my conversation with Steph while I waited to show the police my potential evidence.

After the police left with the bagged face cradle from the massage table in hand, Kimber announced, "I need a snack."

"I know a place. It's almost closing time, but if we hurry…" I started walking with Kimber in tow.

"I can drive us," she said.

"No need," I pointed across and up the street a bit. "It's that little blue house, there."

After the short walk, Kimber slipped Murphy into her oversized purse, and we opened the front door to Penumbra.

The place was empty except for one person, "Gary. Hi."

"Hi, Murphy. Who's your friend?" He extended his hand to Kimber.

As she reached for his hand, he took a step closer to her.

"Kimber," she said with a smile, as she took a step closer to him.

I was getting uncomfortable and it was definitely not jealousy. I picked a table and sat to wait out their introductions. Time was ticking on getting something from the kitchen.

Gary said, "I'm a fellow food critic of Murphy's. How come I haven't seen you around before?"

"Because I'm not from around here," Kimber bubbled.

This was like the worst bar experience I could imagine. And this place didn't even have a liquor license to help me black it out.

"Kimber," I called out from my table. "The kitchen closes soon."

She came over, followed by Gary.

He said, "Don't worry. I know the owner."

"I know the owner, too," I said. *Why was I playing his game?*

Kimber sat down and so did Gary. *And why did I choose a four-top?*

She seemed amused, looking back and forth between the two of us.

"Do you live upstairs, now, Gary?" I asked.

"This is kind of my home away from home, or my office, anyway," he said with a wink to Kimber.

I was never a fan of the guy, and this was reinforcing my judgment. I didn't care if he wanted to take Kimber off my hands, but the smarminess still irked me.

"Kimber and I need to talk, Gary. So, if you don't mind…"

He replied with a smile while looking at her, "No problem. I'll be right over there if you want me."

"We won't," I said.

He walked to a table in the next room and sat in front of a pile of papers.

"He seems like a nice guy," Kimber said.

I was saved from continuing to think about Gary when Chef Burke walked up.

"Mr. Murphy, it's good to see you so soon. Are you ready for some samples from the menu to review?"

I noted that his chef's hat was riding a bit low. I felt bad that we had come in at closing time when he obviously had a tough day.

"Any cinnamon rolls left?" I asked.

"I can warm one up for you." Burke stepped away to the kitchen.

"Only one?" Kimber asked me, with a frown.

"Don't worry, half of one of these cinnamon rolls is more than enough for a snack. Though Gary might buy you one of your own if you'd like to sit with him."

"I can share with you." She feigned hurt feelings. "I don't believe I've read about Penumbra on your blog."

"I don't come here often. The food and service have always been a bit uneven. It can be good, or the toast may show up burnt. I can't recommend it, and don't really need to as the place already has quite the wait on weekends. Besides, Gary has it more than covered."

"What's your deal with Gary?"

"I don't have a 'deal' with Gary. He just gets my goat. His reviews seem dependent on how much free food he's served. It's not the way I do business."

"He seems very friendly."

"I never said he wasn't friendly."

Kimber picked up her fork in one hand and her butter knife in the other. "Which would you choose if you had to defend yourself—a fork or a butter knife?"

"Do I have to defend myself against you? I can order you your own cinnamon roll if you want."

"No, just in general. Would a pointy fork be a better weapon than a dull butter knife?"

"I don't think either would be much of a deterrent, but I guess I would keep the fork and give you the butter knife."

"Ah, then you have fallen into my trap."

"Your trap?"

It was a good thing that the cinnamon roll chose that moment to show up. The chef put it in the middle of the table and set a small plate in front of each of us.

"I'll watch for the review," he said as he left our table.

We each used our fork and knife to make short work of the pastry.

It was warm and gooey, and the frosting was sweet and creamy—it was too bad I wasn't doing reviews anymore.

I left cash on the table as I didn't want to wait for the check, if the chef even planned to give us one. We walked past Gary's table on the way out.

I asked him, "You don't happen to know Conor McCloud, do you?"

"I've seen him around here," he replied and then turned his attention to Kimber. "I would be more than happy to show you around town—take you to one of our finer restaurants that Murphy wouldn't be able to get in."

I was plenty able, I fumed to myself. But let him take her out if she wanted. I had three murders to solve anyway.

Gary gave Kimber his card, and we walked back to her car.

She looked up at me. "I don't need to go out with Gary, but he could have some useful information."

"Gary? Useful information? Those don't go together. He could be the murderer for all I know. But I don't know what his motive would be. Would he want to make me quit the business? I don't think he sees me as any kind of impediment."

"Then maybe I could try to find out his motive," she said.

"If he killed three people, do you think you should go out with him, alone?"

"I can take care of myself." She put a hand on her large purse.

If she thought the fluffy little friend it contained would help, more power to her.

"You're an adult. You do what you want." I left her at her car.

Chapter Twelve

I needed to clear my head, and I was worried about Irma, so I went to check on her.

I spoke to the man at the front counter of the police impound lot. "I'd like to see Irma, please."

"There's nobody here by that name." He didn't look up from his book—a new mystery I hadn't had a chance to read, yet.

"I mean, I would like to see my car."

"Name?"

"Murphy."

He clicked on his computer. "Not gonna happen—it's evidence in the Marie Fuller case."

Nuts. Apparently they weren't done with Irma, yet.

I said, "Thank you," but I wasn't sure he heard me as he had already returned to his novel.

I went back outside and examined the chain-link fence surrounding the lot. It had slats inserted to prevent wandering eyes. I found a broken slat to peek through, and it didn't take long to find my quarry—a classic like Irma was easy to spot a mile away. She was parked in the middle of the only mud puddle in the entire dirt lot.

She looked little the worse for her adventure, which was good—I might need her for a quick getaway from this town of murders. But it could be some time before I could get her back from evidence lockup. I needed to solve at least the last murder to free her.

I spoke through the fence, "I'm sorry about this indignity, Irma. I'm trying to get it cleared up as quickly as possible so I can get you back home. But as of right now, I have three murder victims. This case might be too complicated for a simple food blogger. I wish you could tell me who left that poor woman with you, but I'm not crazy enough to think that this is more than a monologue." *At least, not yet.* One more body, though, could push me over the edge.

I turned and leaned my back against the fence, wondering what my next move should be.

Then I realized the man at the counter had given me the name of the third victim.

Chapter Thirteen

I looked up Marie Fuller on social and found she was a hairstylist. I visited the shop where she had worked—a small place with only two chairs. I spoke to the lone occupant, a woman sweeping, though I saw no hair or other debris on the floor.

"Hello. Mind if I ask you about Marie?"

She put aside the broom and sat down in one of the chairs. She spun it, putting her back to me. "I've already spoken to the cops."

"I'm sure you have, but they're not talking to me."

"Then why should I talk to you?"

"I'm trying to figure out why someone would kill Marie."

"And who are you?"

"Almost nobody at this point—a former food blogger—Murphy."

She spun her chair to face me. "Murphy Slaw? I love that blog."

"Yeah, that was me."

"I'm Felicia. Maybe you've seen me in the comments. You're not giving up your blog, are you?"

"I might have to if I can't get these murders to stop. The police aren't moving fast enough, so I was hoping to find out what I could about Marie."

"You can't quit. I'll try to help, but I've been out of the shop the last couple of days."

"Is it only the two of you who work here?"

"There are three of us—well…were." She spun her chair back away from me.

"Was there anybody you can think of who would want to hurt her?"

"I don't think so," she said to me in the mirror.

"Is there a way I can look at her client list? Do you keep a calendar on the computer?"

She spun in her chair again, facing me. "We use paper calendar books. We block out dates so that only two of us, at most, are scheduled at a time."

"And I suppose the police took her book."

"No, I couldn't find her book when they asked for it. But they might have found it at her apartment."

"Or, her killer might have taken it," I pondered.

"Why would somebody kill her? She was a good person."

I didn't want to tell her that it might be about me—that Marie might have just been collateral damage in a murder spree targeting me. I didn't even want to think it myself.

"That's what I want to find out," I said. "Do you think you can put together a list of her clients that you remember seeing?" I knew it was a breach of client privacy, but I also knew Felicia might prefer it to getting murdered.

"I can do that. I'll ask Jane who she remembers, too."

"Let me run a name by you." It was a long shot, but it was the only other name I had so far. "Do you know if Marie knew a Conor McCloud?"

"We all know him. He's our accountant, and he sucks."

That was to the point. "Why does he suck?"

"You should ask him that. Not only does he make mistakes on our taxes, he charges us to fix them. 'An hour is an hour,' he says. Marie and I have been lobbying Jane to find a new accountant, but for some reason, she won't budge."

"Well, you're going to have to find a new one, now—he's dead."

She gasped. "You don't think Marie killed him and then killed herself, do you?"

Why would she say that? What kind of shows does she watch? It was a possibility, but still, why toss your coworker under the Mountain Metro?

"Did Marie want to kill him?" I asked.

"Only sometimes. He cost her buying a house by screwing up her paperwork for the loan."

So, we have a connection between two of the murders—Marie and McCloud knew each other. And Felicia and Jane knew him as well. Suspects were starting to peek out of the cabinetry. More legwork for me—now I needed to talk to Jane.

"Please contact me at my blog address with the client list, or anything else you think could help. And I would like to chat with Jane, if you would let her know for me."

"I'll do that. Please don't quit your blog."

I smiled at her and wandered back outside into the sunshine.

Chapter Fourteen

It turned out Jane didn't want to chat with me, so I came up with an alternate plan. I was sure Kimber would like to get her hair done, so I made an online appointment for her with Jane.

"What's wrong with my hair?" Kimber demanded when I phoned to tell her my plan.

"Nothing. I'm sure it's lovely." I told her what happened at the salon and about Jane being uncooperative. "You'll have to watch your step— the place could be a den of murderers."

"I said I can take care of myself."

"I'm sure you can." Kimber struck me as someone not to get on the wrong side of. "But still, either one of the hairstylists could have killed either Marie or McCloud, or both, or maybe both killed them, or one killed one and the other killed the other."

"And umbrella guy?"

"I don't know. There are getting to be too many moving parts for me."

"Should I wear a wire?" she asked.

"Do you have a wire?"

"No. Don't you have one?"

"I'm not a spy," I said. "I'm a blogger."

"What will we do, then?"

"We'll have to do it the old-fashioned way—you'll have to tell me what you learn."

Chapter Fifteen

I met Kimber in the lobby of her B&B after she had done the deed.

"What did you find out from Jane?" I asked.

"You didn't compliment me on my new look," she huffed.

Having other things on my mind, like solving three murders, I hadn't noticed her hair.

"Your hair looks nice."

"It's a wonder you're not married."

"I've been married. Did you get anything else from Jane, besides a new look?"

"She had plenty to say about the girls and McCloud. It's amazing what people will tell total strangers."

"Did she tell you why she wanted to keep McCloud on as accountant when he had treated the other women so badly?"

"He was blackmailing her with her own personal information."

"So, she was in a sticky situation," I contemplated aloud. "Her partners wanted to fire him but she couldn't let them because he would turn her in for tax fraud or some such. He was a real standup guy. If he treated all his clients like that, it was only a matter of time till he turned up dead."

"It gave Jane motive to end his racket, permanently," Kimber said.

"Let's not forget, Marie still had motive, too. He had treated her badly as well, and she was also stuck with him."

"I don't know that Marie would kill him. Jane raved about her partners and felt bad that she couldn't let them fire McCloud."

"If we hypothesize that Jane killed McCloud, would she have killed Marie as well?" I had a whole list of questions. "Could Marie have figured out that Jane had killed him and had to be silenced herself? And what about a connection to umbrella guy? Was he possibly a client, or were the murders unrelated? I wish I knew if we had one, two, or even three or more killers."

"At least there haven't been any new murders."

"That we know of," I lamented.

"You're in a mood."

Three bodies. My career hanging in the balance. A small dog trying to lick my face. I was in a mood.

Chapter Sixteen

It was time I tried to find out more about Conor McCloud. I went to his place of business to see what I could dredge up, leaving Kimber at her B&B to admire and tweak her new look.

Upon entering the old Victorian that had been converted to house several businesses, I spotted a gentleman sitting in an office with an open door. The plaque outside the office listed two names—Conor McCloud and Peter Wystrop. I spoke to whom I supposed was the latter.

"Mr. Wystrop, I'd like to extend my condolences to you."

"Thank you. You must be one of Conor's clients. I'll be emailing everyone with options for their accounts."

"I'm not one of his clients. I'm looking into his death."

"Are you now? I have no time for someone from the paper or the intersphere or wherever you're from."

I supposed I was from the intersphere, as he put it.

"I won't take up much of your time. Is it possible to look at Mr. McCloud's client list?"

"Our client list is confidential," he told me. "Please close the door on your way out."

"But the police have a copy?"

"A warrant will do that."

"Can you at least tell me if he was having a problem with anyone?"

"Why would I do that? You're just some guy that comes walking in off the street and starts asking personal questions about confidential matters."

That was me. I wondered if it would help if I told him I was a food blogger.

"How many people work here?" I asked.

He just stared at me.

"Surely you can tell me that."

"There were only the two of us, plus a part-time office assistant. Now, please leave. As you can imagine, I have a lot of work to do."

The bridge seemed burned, so blowing it up shouldn't make it any worse. "Did you tell the police about McCloud's extortion sideline, or is that something you plan to continue?"

This time, he glared at me. Maybe it did make it worse.

"Does that mean you didn't know about the shakedowns?" I pressed.

"I have no idea what you are talking about, nor do I want to know. Go or I will invite the police back."

A different tack, then. "Okay. Thank you for talking with me. Before I go, may I ask where you get your hair done?"

He looked up at me and smiled. "Do you like it? I had them take a bit of the gray out. It's a small barbershop downtown. I think I have their card around here somewhere."

He searched his desk drawer and then presented me with a business card.

"Thank you," I said. "I'll be sure to check them out."

I left, closing the door behind me, as he had asked. I reviewed the business card—not the shop where Marie had worked, but that didn't necessarily mean he had no connection to her demise.

As for his late partner, Wystrop might have discovered McCloud's side business and realized it wasn't good for their shared business. The only sure solution would be to liquidate McCloud. He didn't seem broken up at all about the death. And adding McCloud's clients to his own would be a windfall. Peter Wystrop could have even been a blackmail victim himself—motives everywhere, I mused.

I made a mental note to look into the part-time office assistant. What kind of sleuth would I be if they turned out to be the killer after a quick mention and no further consideration?

Chapter Seventeen

I was relieved to answer a call from Dave.

"Am I off time-out?" I asked.

"No, not at all. I'm supposed to pass along a message and then zip it. My boss wants you out of town—you're getting in the way of the investigation."

"Surely, he doesn't think I killed any of them? That I would leave the bodies in my own wake, to get what—fodder for my blog? That I would leave a victim in my own car because he would know I was too smart to ever do that?"

Dave said, "Let's say that while you might not be at the top of the list, that doesn't mean you're not on the list."

"I thought suspects weren't supposed to leave town. What if they decide they want to arrest me?"

"They figure you're pretty easy to find since you always put where you are on your blog."

"I'm not updating my blog right now. Besides, I can't go anywhere with Irma in lockup. Can you spring her?"

"I can't. You'll have to find another way."

"And if I don't?" I shuffled my phone to the other ear.

"Look, Murph. I can only do so much to protect you—to keep you from sharing Irma's fate and be locked up. Don't you have some restaurant away from here you need to go review?"

"I do. But I might be reconsidering my career. Anyway, I would still need wheels."

"Fine. You can borrow my sedan. I can drive my 4x4 till the case is solved."

"Do I need to tell you where I am at all times?"

"No, my car will tell me where you go."

That was convenient. It also meant that Dave would know I didn't go anywhere.

I tried to redirect the conversation. "Can you at least tell me if the leads I gave the police about the peanut butter on the massage table or the comments on my blog posts about doing my job went anywhere?"

There was silence for a long time, but I didn't have anywhere to be.

"They haven't been able to identify who posted the comments, yet. But the peanut butter was poisoned."

So, it wasn't a nut allergy. "What kind of poison?"

"Goodbye, Murph."

Chapter Eighteen

I sat in the driver's seat of the car Dave had dropped off at the house, contemplating my fate. He had only said "Phone" to me, added the car key to it, and walked away.

Kimber pulled up in her rental car and parked behind. She opened the door to my loaner and sat next to me. Her usual happy-go-lucky, flamboyantly-dressed self, she took little Murphy from her purse and put him in the back seat. I hoped the white upholstery was up to the challenge.

"Nice choice," she said. "Did they give you much for Irma?"

"Very funny. I wouldn't trade in a family member. Dave lent it to me. You might as well go home, Kimber. The cops want me out of their way, so I'm supposed to leave town."

"Where should we go? There's nothing waiting for me at home. How about Cabo?"

Mexico? With Kimber? The thought would never cross my mind.

"No, I want to solve the case. I want to get Irma home. I want my life back. I don't want to live in fear of another body dump. By the way, Dave did give me one tiny piece of info—the peanut butter on the massage table was poisoned—McCloud was poisoned. Murphy did a fine job of detective work."

Kimber's eyes widened and her face turned white as jicama.

"What's wrong?" I asked.

She threw her arms around me. "You saved his life! I could have lost Murphy forever." She tightened her grip on me and let out a sob.

I couldn't take credit for that. I was trying to save the evidence. But it would have been devastating for Kimber if something had happened to her little buddy.

Murphy, ignorant of the demise he had ducked, nosed around the back of the big sedan. He jumped into the front to show his mother what he had found—a ball of crumpled paper. Kimber released me and took it from his mouth.

He looked at her insistently. She tossed the crumpled ball into the back seat. Murphy happily fetched it, and the process repeated. Until I finally intervened.

"What is that?" I asked.

Kimber smoothed the paper, then showed me the photo on it. "Is this umbrella guy?"

I grabbed the paper from her. "It could be. It says his name is Juan Carrillo, and it shows an address. Buckle up—we're going to Pueblo. It's not Cabo, but there are some fine Mexican eateries there."

"I thought you weren't supposed to work on the case?"

"They want me out of town, I'm going out of town, if only for the day." I knew this wasn't their intention, but I wasn't about to go on vacation in the middle of a case, or three.

Kimber snatched the paper back from me. "Do you think Dave left this for you to find?"

"It's hard to say. I know he doesn't want to get fired, so we'll assume it fell out of his work bag."

Kimber told the address to the car and we were on our way south. A comfortable silence enrobed us as we cruised down I-25. Murphy dozed in his mother's lap. It had been some time since I had been on a family-style road trip.

As we passed Colorado City, Kimber announced, "I'm thinking about calling Gary."

"Gary?"

"You know, your BFF?"

"I know Gary, but why tell me? You're a grownup, you can date whoever you want." If she was trying to make me jealous, she failed, even if my tone seemed to belie that.

"I thought I might be able to find out if he could be the killer, as you seem to believe."

"I don't know he's the killer. I just know he's shady. But if he is the killer, going on a date with him might not be a good idea."

"Really? Yet you sent me to see Jane, who very well could be the killer. All by myself. Alone with her. To the place where her shopmate had likely been killed. By scissors. Which were everywhere."

That I did. "That sounds like a stupid thing to do when you put it that way. But you told me you could take care of yourself."

"I can."

The car got quiet again until we had nearly reached Pueblo. I wanted to take the chill off and knew just the place.

"Lunch?" I asked Kimber.

"Always."

"Presenting Desert Blossom, one of my favorite cantinas in Colorado," I declared to her as we pulled into the parking lot.

"Are you going to review it for your blog while we're here?" she asked.

"My blog is dead, so no."

"Your blog will live on, even if you don't."

Dark humor aside, she was right, unless I deleted everything. Or maybe she meant she would steal it and carry on in my place. I was never quite sure with Kimber.

We found a table, and a server brought us the customary chips and salsa.

I told Kimber, "This is one of my favorite salsas of any place I've been. And the chips are a perfect match for it."

"That is saying a lot," she offered.

"It really is. Every place I've been, that isn't a chain, has unique chips and salsa. The best places make their own chips, fresh, from their own tortillas, rather than using packaged ones. This place has red and blue corn chips in addition to the traditional yellow or white you might find elsewhere."

"Wow, you should write restaurant reviews or something."

I ignored her. "And the salsa must be fresh, as well. Of course, not everyone might agree with my particular taste."

"Your very particular taste, indeed." She seemed to be relishing this.

So I pressed on. "Some people might not like a forceful cilantro presence, for example. And then there is the heat level."

"Yes, there is always the heat level. Do go on." She fanned her face with her hand.

"I like a low to moderate heat level to my salsa. Too much heat and you can blow out your taste buds and not enjoy the rest of the meal. But there needs to be some heat to it. It can't only be chopped vegetables."

"No one would want that."

We both busted out laughing, and that was before the Margaritas.

Chapter Nineteen

After lunch, we made our way to the address on the paper we had found in Dave's car. It could have been a dead end, but it got me out of town, per Dave's boss's wishes. Well, I was sure he didn't wish I went out of town to follow a lead.

Kimber stuffed Murphy into her purse, and we went up the concrete walk. I knocked on the front door of the modest bungalow, and a middle-aged woman in a flowered dress answered.

"Hello," I said, holding up the paper from the car. "Do you know this man?"

"No English," she replied in a heavy accent and hurried to close the door on us.

I had picked up a little Spanish from hanging out in restaurant kitchens, but not enough to carry on a conversation, much less conduct an interview. A dead end it was.

Before the woman could get the door shut and I could turn back to the car, Kimber said, "*Yo hablo español.*"

The woman sighed and opened the door wide. "Come in," she said, in perfect English.

"*Gracias,*" I said as we entered her small living room.

I held up the paper with the picture again, and she pushed it down out of her view.

"I already told the police I don't know anything."

"We're not with the police." I noticed a guy a little younger than the victim in the next room, eating a tamale. "Would he know the man?"

The woman turned and waved at him. "*Salte.*"

The young man jumped up, and I heard a screen door slap the house. We were getting nowhere.

Kimber spoke up, "Mr. Murphy here found this man's body. Are you sure you don't know him?"

She looked at me, her eyes welling up, "You're the one who found Gabriel?"

"Sadly, I am. Did you know him well?"

"He was my nephew. Can you tell me what happened to him? His mother has been anxious to know."

"I'm afraid I can't tell you much. I found him wrapped up in a restaurant umbrella. It looked like he was hit on the head." I didn't want to get too graphic with the grieving woman.

She pulled a tissue from a box near the sofa and sat down.

Kimber sat down next to her. "Is there anything you can tell us about Gabriel that could help us find out who did this to him?"

"It was best I didn't know."

"He was here illegally?" I asked.

The aunt nodded. "I believe he worked in a restaurant up north. He gave me money to send to my sister sometimes. It smelled like *tocino*."

Kimber mouthed the translation to me, but I already knew it was bacon. I could speak food in many languages.

We extended our sympathies to Gabriel's aunt and thanked her for her time.

I pointed Dave's car toward home, and Kimber and I chatted about what we had learned.

She said, "Gabriel, very likely worked in a restaurant. It could have been Fash Food."

"But Rudy said he didn't know him," I countered.

"And a killer would never lie, right? Besides, you said Gabriel wasn't all that recognizable at the time. Or maybe Rudy doesn't know all the help."

"You do know you're raising more questions than you're answering. But, yes. It does make sense to go back to Fash Food and do some reconnaissance. It might not be Rudy, but the killer could be close by."

Kimber thoughtfully added, "Then again, if the killer was out to get you, they might have brought the body from further north, like Denver, to leave it for you."

"Thanks for that. I feel so much better now."

She was right, though. If the body was some kind of message to me, it could have come from anywhere. But we couldn't check everywhere. The fact that Gabriel was undocumented from south of the border working in a restaurant kitchen did little to prune the field. The best we could do was start close to home and work our way out from there.

"In any case, Fash Food is closed now—we'll have to go in the morning."

"In the meantime," Kimber said, "let's try to narrow down our suspect list. To make it simpler, let's say there's a single killer. They would have to know a fair bit about your life."

"Okay, I'll play along. The killer would have to know where I have brunch on Sunday to leave me the first body. But that one's easy since I've mentioned it on my blog several times. As for the third victim, left at my house, you found my address, which means anyone could."

"So far, we have narrowed it down to everybody."

I pushed past her sarcasm, "The key could be the second victim, Conor McCloud. The killer not only had to know that I frequented the massage place, but the exact day and time of my next appointment. And I have never mentioned any of that in my blog."

"We have to consider that McCloud's timing could be coincidental, or even unrelated," Kimber posed.

"It could very well be a coincidence. I would prefer not to have been hacked. But that might indicate a second killer, something we're not contemplating at the moment," I pointed out. "Since knowing about my life got us nowhere, let's try to discern a motive."

"Motive for the murders or for dropping the bodies at your feet?"

"Exactly. What if the victims were random, merely fodder for the actual goal of getting to me?"

Kimber picked up the ball. "Let's consider that. What would someone have to gain? They don't seem to have gone so far as trying to pin the murders on you. Is their motivation money? Is it love? Has someone you jilted in your past suddenly deemed it time you pay the price? Or someone more current, perhaps?"

"If that's your convoluted way of asking if I'm seeing anyone, I am not. As for the past, I would hope I would not have created so much animosity that an old love murdered three people to get back at me. Heaven forbid that I would have dated someone capable of doing that."

"Money, then. How does someone gain financially from what you do?"

"A good review can help entice new people to a restaurant they may not have tried, or remind them of one they hadn't been to lately. But, again, three murders for a good review?"

"Three, so far."

"That's incredibly helpful of you to bring up."

"What else, then?" she asked.

"Maybe they want to be caught—"

"By the illustrious murder-solving food blogger. They would get to be highlighted in your blog for all time."

I winced. "They should leave better clues if they want to get caught by me. Dave is right.

Getting out of town could give the cops more time to find the killer and end the killing spree."

Kimber said, "I think we should look along the other road, first—that the victims were the targets and you were just an enhancement to the plan."

"An enhancement?"

"Sure, like a good glass of wine with a steak dinner," she elaborated.

"I could go for either of those. In the meantime, I think that line of reasoning makes the most sense. They had people to kill, and why not spoil my day while they're at it?"

We arrived back at my place.

Kimber piped up, "I don't know how to tell you this, but I'm hungry again. How about another half of a cinnamon roll?"

"Sure. Penumbra should be quiet now."

Chapter Twenty

I went into my house for a pitstop while Kimber took Murphy on a short walk for the same.

My phone told me Dave was calling. I felt more than a little guilty about the deed we had done in his car, but I answered anyway, instead of letting it go to voicemail.

"My car says you're in town," he said. "You're supposed to stay away from here."

"Sorry, Dave, but I don't take orders from your superiors. One of the beauties of the blogging life is I get to be my own boss."

"I see you've been to Pueblo. Any reason?"

"I wanted Kimber to try the salsa at Desert Blossom. It's a favorite."

"That's the only reason?"

"Should there be another? By the way, I have the real name of the first victim, if you want it."

Dave took the name. I didn't know where he would tell his boss he got it from.

Chapter Twenty-One

Quiet Penumbra was, as in completely empty. Even Gary was nowhere to be seen. Kimber and I sat at what was becoming our usual table and continued our crime-solving chat while waiting for someone to take our order.

I picked up where we had left off. "Each of the victims must have been a problem for the killer in some way."

Kimber speculated, "Suppose the first victim, Gabriel, worked in a kitchen—he could have been terrible at his job. But it should have been easy to fire him, especially if he was undocumented. He would have no recourse."

"What would stop you from firing someone?"

"Maybe they were family? Or maybe they had something on me."

"Do tell. What would someone have on you?" I asked.

She gave me side-eye. "We know the second victim, McCloud, was a blackmailer, so money as the motive is definitely in play there. The third victim, Marie, was a hairstylist. The three victims were all so different."

"Don't forget that Marie knew McCloud, too. The killer may have been a little too chatty during a haircut. Marie may have put two and two together and cost herself her life."

"It sounds like we're sneaking up on some motives, but do we have a suspect that fits?"

I took my shot. "Let's start with Gary."

"Why is he at the top of the list?"

I presented my evidence. "Gary admitted to knowing McCloud, and he must get haircuts."

"It sounds like you're reaching. We don't know for sure that he knew Gabriel or Marie."

"Fine. There are Jane and Felicia from the hair styling shop."

Kimber added, "We have Steph, the massage therapist."

"And also, the partner at the accounting firm, Peter Wystrop. Plus, Rudy or someone else at Fash Food, where it all began. Can I finally add Gary at the end of the list?"

"You can, but it seems awfully childish. Have we given up considering that one of the later victims killed one of the earlier victims?"

"That's still a possibility, but I think we need to focus on finding a live killer."

"Something we haven't considered is that two of the bodies were moved from where they were killed. Hoisting Gabriel up into that umbrella must have taken some effort," Kimber pointed out.

"Steph seems fairly strong, and the two hairstylists could have been working together. I'm not sure that lets anyone off the hook."

Kimber said, "We need to remember that the killer has some connection to you—some grudge against you that is causing them to leave the victims at your doorstep, so to speak."

"Gary does," I volunteered.

Kimber gave me a wry look. "What about the women at the beauty shop?"

"I've never been in there and don't think I knew any of them. And I haven't done any business with the accounting firm, either."

"Then I'm afraid we'll have to take a good look at Steph, your massage therapist. She knows your schedule and probably your address."

"She does. I'm also certain I have mentioned my regular brunch to her. I don't like where this is going."

"Can you think of any motive for her to do this to you, or the three victims?"

"Only McCloud—Steph could easily be another of his blackmail targets. He apparently even coerced her into letting him nap after a massage. But why kill him in her own shop? Even with the other two murders, she would be the prime suspect in his death."

"Not all killers think things through. Maybe she thought the poison would take longer to work, and he wouldn't die on the spot."

"I'll tell you what, Kimber, I'll move her to the top of the list, but I don't feel good about it. It feels like we don't have enough suspects. There could be so many connections that I'm not seeing.

I think I may have bitten off more than I can chew trying to solve three murders at the same time."

"Your track record maintains you can do this," Kimber offered.

She was right—I had to keep pushing. "I have a hunch that Conor McCloud is the real bad guy here, setting this whole sequence of events in motion, somehow."

Chef Burke chose that moment to come out of the kitchen to greet us.

"You talking about that blackmailing weasel, McCloud?" he asked.

"You know him?" I responded.

"I am familiar with his work."

"We're trying to figure out who killed him," Kimber volunteered.

The chef shot me a steely look. "That is a job for the police. Don't you have your own job to do? I'm still waiting for your cinnamon roll review."

Kimber piped up again, "We're back for another taste, if that helps."

"No. No more food for either of you. I'm past tired of people not doing their jobs."

I was starting to get the idea we'd missed a prime suspect for our list. A little more prodding might seal the deal.

"So, you were a client of McCloud's?" I asked.

"A client, a mark—it was all the same to him. He did a lousy job on my books but a stellar one ferreting out my indiscretions. His elimination did the world a favor."

Possibly. But Burke still hadn't admitted that he did the eliminating.

"Did Gabriel Hernandez, aka Juan Castillo, work here?" I continued my inquisition.

"Many cooks have passed through my kitchen."

I took that as a yes. "Did you know he was in the country illegally?"

"You mean, did I care?"

I guess I did. This had probably gone far enough, maybe too far. He was right—we should leave him to the police.

I stood up. "We should get going. C'mon, Kimber."

She grabbed her purse and stood.

"But you haven't gotten your just desserts," Burke said, even though he had rebuked Kimber's earlier request. From under his apron, he produced the biggest butcher knife I'd ever seen—it looked like a small sword.

"Run, Kimber." I pushed her towards the door.

She dashed for it and was free. I was blocked from following her by a madman, expertly wielding a tool of his trade. I stepped back against the wall, putting a table between us.

"So, I'm next," I said.

"You're as useless to me as the rest of them. Why couldn't you simply do your job?"

I didn't think a description of my culinary experiences in his establishment would cause him to relent. "Kimber will bring the police."

"Let her. By then, you'll be dead and I'll be gone."

So, what he was telling me was that I had better stall for time. "I see you wanting to get rid of McCloud, but why 86 Gabriel?"

"He was working with McCloud, sharing the spoils, and giving me attitude. A cast iron skillet to the back of the head put him face down on the grill—a nice happenstance that made him hard to ID till I got to McCloud. Didn't want to tip off that crook that he was next."

"And the hairstylist?" I noted his chef's hat was still riding low. "Certainly, a bad haircut doesn't call for an execution. Hair grows back."

He threw his hat to the floor. "Hair does, but ears don't."

The top third of his right ear had been sheared off. *Ouch.*

Burke pushed the table hard against me, pinning me to the wall. Lying in front of me were a butter knife and a fork—both diminutive in contrast to his weapon. I picked one up in each hand, anyway. I had no idea what Kimber would do with them and merely crossed the utensils in front of me. Where was she when I needed her?

Chef Burke drew back his big knife and thrust it toward my chest.

My eyes were fixed on the approaching silver blade. This guy had already killed three people. What chance did I have against him? I had gone too far. Rather than dropping my blog, focusing on it instead of trying to solve crimes could have saved my life and possibly the lives of others.

A loud bang shook me from my stupor. The chef's knife flew wide of me and stuck into the wooden floor as Burke's head smacked the table.

I then saw Kimber behind him, revolver in her hands. She slid down the wall behind her to sit cross-legged on the ground. She laid the gun down and wept.

"Kimber! Are you okay?"

She nodded. "I've never killed anybody before."

I reached across the table and felt the chef's neck for a pulse, careful to avoid his bloodied shoulder.

"You're in luck—you still haven't. I'll call 911."

"I already did," she said, "before I came back for you."

I could now hear sirens in the distance. "Thank you for that—coming back, I mean. I don't think I would have escaped this time. I'm sorry I put you in danger. It won't happen again."

"I told you I could take care of myself."

Chapter *Fin*

The following morning, Dave came to collect his car from my care.

"We good?" he asked.

"Of course we're good," I replied. "I'm still working on whether or not I'm good. Maybe a stiff ocean breeze would help clear my mind."

"I did suggest you get out of town. C'mon, I'll take you to spring Irma."

Driving back home from the impound lot where Dave had dropped me, I spotted Kimber giving Murphy a final walk around the neighborhood before leaving town. I parked Irma at the curb and joined them.

She smiled. "Hi, Murph. Or bye, Murph."

"I'm glad I caught you before you left," I said. "I wanted to tell you how grateful I am for all your help, and for saving me."

"You saved my Murphy—consider us even." Her pup looked up at the sound of his name and then returned to his business. "So, did your life pass before your eyes?"

"Only the dumbest moments."

We walked past Penumbra on the way back to her car. I expected the place to be shuttered, but Gary was out front, wearing a chef's hat and setting the patio tables.

"Hi, Kimber, Murphy," he said.

"Hello, Gary," she said. "I'm sorry I didn't get the chance to call you before I leave town."

"Next time," he said. "I'll be right here."

I had to ask, "Why will you be right here—I mean at Penumbra?"

"Burke wanted me to take over for him while he's in the hospital," he said. "And I was here anyway."

"You do know he's never coming back," I observed.

Gary shrugged his shoulders, and Kimber and I walked on.

We arrived at her car and she slid in. She put Murphy on the passenger seat and looked up at me from the open driver's door. "You can't give it up, you know."

"I won't be giving up my blog."

"No, I mean crime solving. It's in your gut as much as your favorite salsa and chips. You'll never be able to quit it."

Maybe she was right. But it would be a long time before I was ready to confront a killer again. "And how are you doing? You said you had never shot anyone before."

"I said I had never killed anybody. I'll be fine, Murph." She closed her car door and drove away.

Murph's Chocolate Cinnamon Cookies

These double-chocolatey cinnamon cookies provide a bit of heat from ginger instead of the customary chili powder, for a unique spin on a south-of-the-border favorite.

1½ cups all-purpose flour

¼ cup cocoa powder

2 teaspoons cinnamon

1 teaspoon ground ginger

½ teaspoon baking soda

¼ teaspoon salt

½ cup (1 stick) unsalted butter, softened

½ cup light brown sugar

½ cup white sugar

1 egg

1 teaspoon vanilla extract

½ cup semi-sweet chocolate chips

Whisk together the dry ingredients—flour, cocoa powder, cinnamon, ginger, baking soda, and salt—in a bowl and set aside. Cream the butter and sugars. Mix in the egg and vanilla. Mix in the set-aside dry ingredients in two or three portions. Mix in the chocolate chips.

Form the batter into uniform-sized balls—smaller for more cookies, larger for more substantial cookies—and refrigerate for an hour. Preheat the oven to 350 degrees. Bake for about 10 minutes.

Pro tip: Substitute cinnamon chips for half the chocolate chips and reduce cinnamon to 1 teaspoon.

Thank you for reading *Cracked: A Snack-Sized Mystery.* We hope you enjoyed the ride. Please leave a review on Amazon and/or Goodreads, and tell your friends.

Join Murph on all his culinary adventures:
Smoked: A Snack-Sized Mystery (1)
Cracked: A Snack-Sized Mystery (2)
Tossed: A Snack-Sized Mystery *Cruise* (3)
Squashed: A Snack-Sized Mystery (4)
Toasted: A Snack-Sized Mystery *Wedding* (5)

More at JmarsInk.com.

About the Author

Jeff Schmoyer tries to find humor in the crazy world around him. Several of his short plays have been produced, and his short stories have been published in the Pikes Peak Writers anthologies, *Journeys into Possibility* and *The Other Side of the Mountain*. He is the author of the **Snack-Sized Mystery** series starring food blogger Murph Murphy, including *Smoked, Cracked, Tossed, Squashed,* and *Toasted*. He is always up for a tasty meal and a friendly game of cards. Find more at JmarsInk.com.